ITTY BITTY KITTY

Joan Holub
Illustrated by James Burks

HARPER
An Imprint of HarperCollins*Publishers*

iTTY BiTTY

For Barbara, who rescued itty-bitty adorable Ollie —J.H.

For my Granny—I love and miss you —J.B.

Itty Bitty Kitty

Copyright © 2015 by HarperCollins Publishers.

All rights reserved. Manufactured in China.

No part of this book may be used or reproduced in any manner whatsoever without written permission except in the case of brief quotations embodied in critical articles and reviews.

For information address HarperCollins Children's Books, a division of HarperCollins Publishers, 195 Broadway, New York, NY 10007.

www.harpercollinschildrens.com

ISBN 978-0-06-232219-7

The artist used Photoshop CS5 with a Wacom Cintiq monitor to create the digital illustrations for this book.

Typography by Joe Merkel

15 16 17 18 19   SCP   10 9 8 7 6 5 4 3 2 1

❖

First Edition

"Mom? Dad? Can I get a cat?" asked Ava. "Pretty, pretty, pleasey, weasey, I'll take good care of it, with sugar on top?"

Dad looked doubtful. "Cats shed."

Mom shook her head. "Cats must be regularly fed."

And no matter how much Ava begged, their answer did not change.

"No pet!" said Mom.

"Not yet," said Dad. "Maybe when you're older."

Ava stomped down the hall
and clomped down the steps

to mope in the seat at the end of her street.

Mew.

Suddenly, she heard an itty-bitty sound.

It was a furry purry,
snuggly huggly,
cutie patootie,

itty...

bitty...

kitty!

He had sparkly green eyes
and was just the right size
for a girl like Ava.

FREE Kitten

"You can be my kitty! I will name you Itty Bitty."
Ava scooped him up and ran home, hoping Mom
and Dad would let her keep him.

But Mom and Dad were still in a "no" kind of mood.
The puppy next door was going crazy in Mom's daisies.
And Dad was going bananas with work.

Ava tiptoed to her room.
"I'd better hide you for a while," she whispered.
"You will be my itty-bitty secret."

Itty Bitty was a very good kitty.
He was good at dress-up,

CLAP
CLAP

. . . at pajama parties,

. . . and at pouncing.

Ava was good at taking care of Itty Bitty.
"Mom and Dad will soon see that I'm *not*
too little to have a cat."

There was just one problem with her new kitty.
After only one week, he was no longer exactly itty.

Luckily, Mom and Dad didn't suspect a thing.

And after a second week passed,
Ava's kitty was neither itty nor bitty.

PRRRRRRR!

He flicked when he licked.

He squashed when he washed.

He squished when he swished.

CRUNCH

One morning, Itty Bitty woke up feeling frisky.
His paws went hurry scurry.
Before Ava could stop him, he dashed off
through the house!

Where he . . .

scared the fish,
broke a dish,
chased a bug,
clawed the rug,
leaped from a cupboard,

CRACK

and got DISCOVERED!

"Call the zoo!" yelled Dad.
"Call the cat-catcher," shouted Mom.
"No! Wait!" cried Ava. "You can just *call* him Itty Bitty. He's our new kitty!"

Dad looked doubtful. "He's way too tall and long."
Mom shook her head. "He's altogether wrong!"
"His name might be Itty Bitty, but he's too much kitty!
Tomorrow, he has to go."

And that was that.

That night, Ava held Itty Bitty tight,
hoping her hugs just might . . .
somehow, some way, change things.
"Oh, Itty Bitty, I wish they could see
that you're really just right."

Then, when everyone was asleep, there came a soft cry that only Itty Bitty's big ears heard.

Waaah!

Itty Bitty padded into the hall.
When he saw the baby, his eyes grew round.
He let out a big fat:

MEE-OWWW!

When baby saw the kitty, he let out an itty-bitty *"Goo?"*

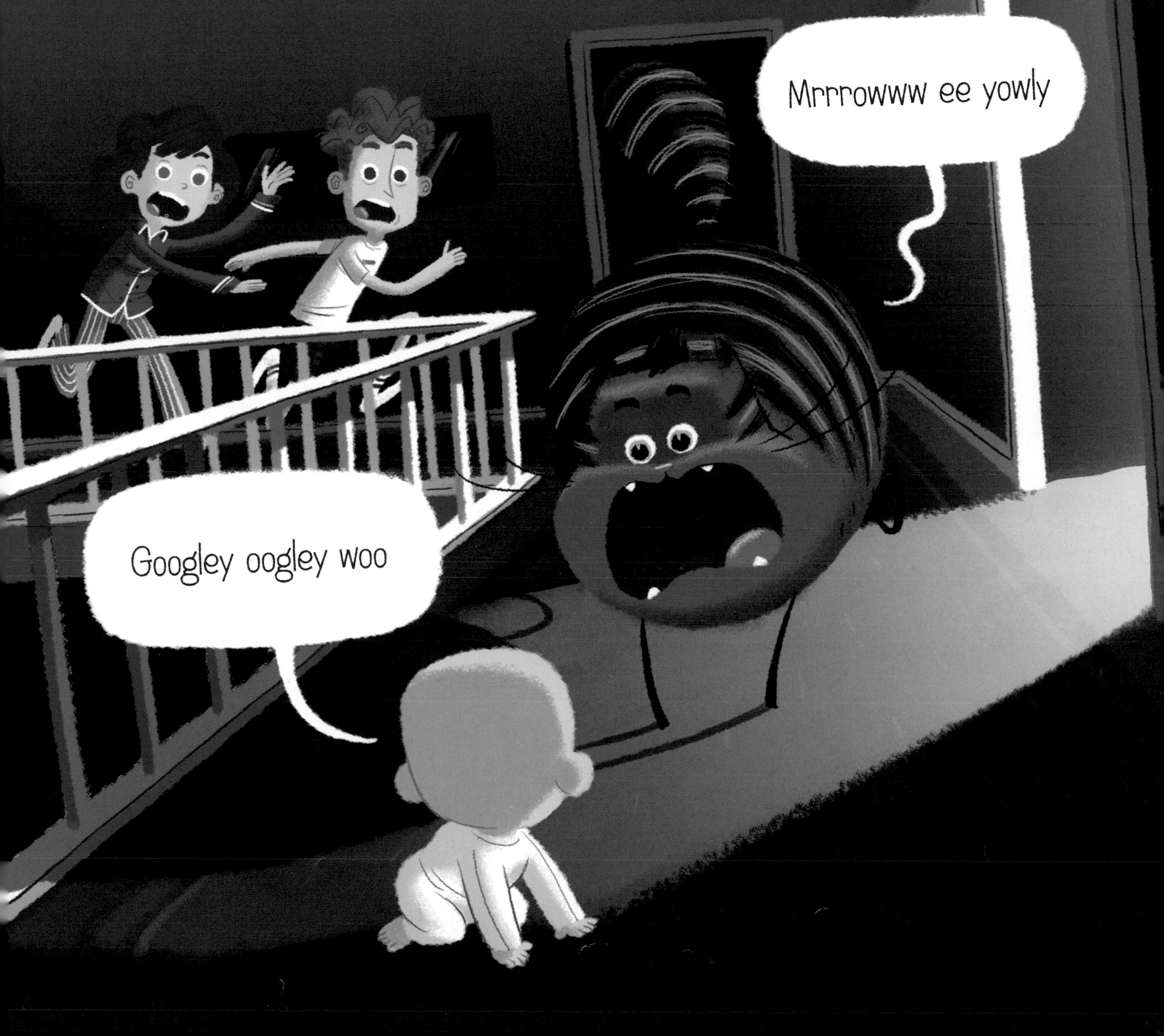

"Thank you, Itty Bitty!" said Mom.
"You saved our baby," said Dad.
Their hearts opened more than an itty-bitty bit wider
to let Ava's new kitty tiptoe inside.

"Maybe," said Mom, "this nose-kissing kitty is just what our family is missing."

"Maybe," said Dad, "this cat is not too long and tall for us after all."

"Can we keep him?" Ava asked, hardly daring to hope.

"Yes," said Mom and Dad.
Ava thought that was the
purrfect answer.